Always My Dad

by Sharon Dennis Wyeth · illustrated by Raúl Colón

An Apple Soup Book

An Imprint of Alfred A. Knopf · New York

For Gary, Brian, Kevin, and our dad, Creed Dennis, Jr.
—S. W.

For Edie, Brian, and Brandon
—R. C.

A note about the art: The illustrations for this book were done using watercolor, charcoal, colored pencils, and lithograph pencils on Fabriano watercolor paper, and etched with tools including an empty ballpoint pen and a scratcher.

17.27   12/10/96

APPLE SOUP IS A TRADEMARK OF ALFRED A. KNOPF, INC.

Text copyright © 1995 by Sharon Dennis Wyeth
Illustrations copyright © 1995 by Raúl Colón

All rights reserved under International and Pan-American Copyright Conventions. Published in the United States of America by Alfred A. Knopf, Inc., New York, and simultaneously in Canada by Random House of Canada Limited, Toronto. Distributed by Random House, Inc., New York.
Book design by Edward Miller

Library of Congress Cataloging-in-Publication Data

Wyeth, Sharon Dennis.
Always my Dad / by Sharon Dennis Wyeth ; illustrated by Raúl Colón.
p.   cm.
"An Apple Soup Book"
Summary: Although she does not get to see her father very often, a girl enjoys the time she and her brothers spend with him one summer while they are visiting their grandparents' farm.
ISBN 0-679-83447-8 (trade) — ISBN 0-679-93447-2 (lib. bdg.)
[1. Fathers—Fiction. 2. Grandparents—Fiction.]   I. Colón, Raúl, ill. II. Title.
PZ7.W9746A1   1995   [E]—dc20   93-43755

Manufactured in the United States of America
2 4 6 8 0 9 7 5 3 1

SOMETIMES the person I want to see more than anyone in the world is my dad. But I only see my dad once in a while.

Daddy moves around a lot, so his address keeps changing. His job keeps changing too. A long time ago he flew planes for the Air Force, and after that he worked in an office. Once, his job was painting houses, and then he fixed televisions. I'm not sure what he does now.

One day last summer Mom took me and my three brothers
to the country to stay with Grandma and Grandpa. They live on a
farm, and they're my dad's mom and dad.

After Mom left us to drive back to the city, I looked around
everywhere—in the barn, in the garden, even in the henhouse. In
the barn I saw Grandpa milking Brownie, and my favorite horse,
Sir Imp, was munching some hay.

When I opened the door to the henhouse, two big hens flew out. Grandma had to run to catch them before they dug up the flowers. Who I was really hoping to see was my dad. I thought maybe he had come to the farm too and was planning to surprise us.

But Daddy wasn't there.

During the day Gary, Brian, Kevin, and I would play hide-and-seek and statues. We helped Grandpa weed the vegetable garden and Grandma pick blackberries in the woods at the edge of the field. "Mind you don't pull up a carrot," Grandpa warned.

"I reckon you little rascals eat more berries than you pick!" Grandma teased, smiling.

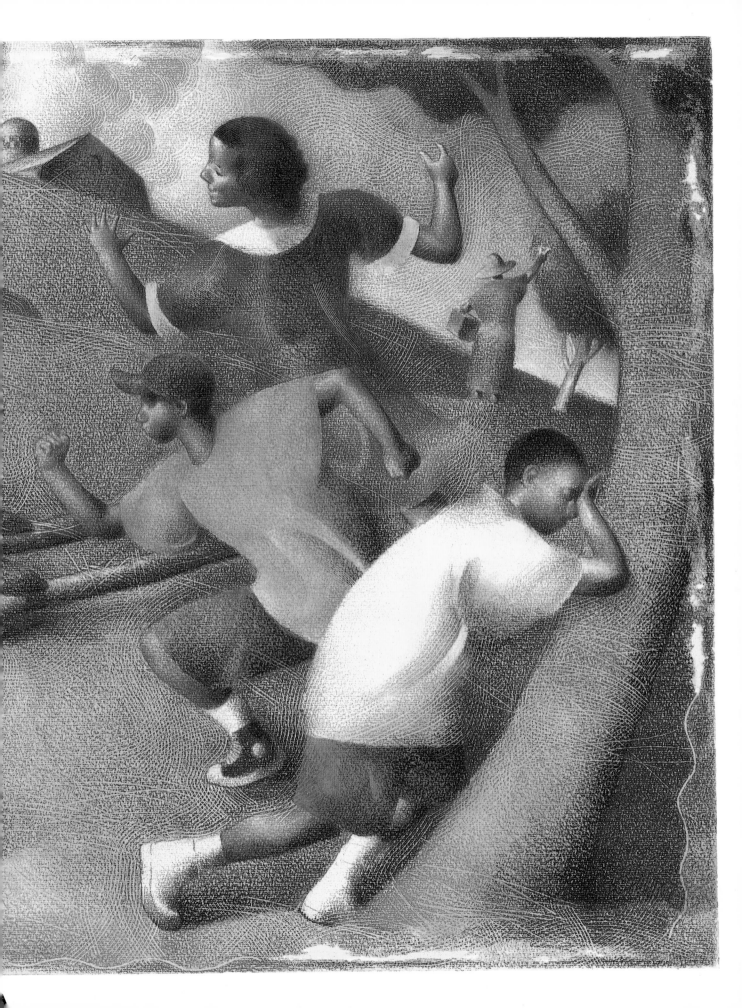

When evening came, we'd listen to peepers on the front porch while we ate our dessert—blackberry cobbler with ice cream. "So peaceful," Grandma would always say. "Just look at that sky."

Sometimes there was a moon with no stars. Sometimes there was a moon and stars together. One special night there was a flickering light on the path that led to the porch.

"Looks like we got a visitor," said Grandpa. Even in the dark from far away I could tell who it was!

"Daddy! Daddy!" My brothers began shouting and running, but suddenly I got shy.

"Hi, Daddy," I said, walking up to him, real slow. He lifted me right up and kissed me on the cheek.

"Hi, sugar," he said. "It's been such a while! Look how tall you've gotten!"

Now each morning, instead of brushing our teeth in the bathroom, we brushed them outside at the pump. Daddy said it was more fun. Instead of wearing shoes, Daddy let us go barefoot. We took rides on Sir Imp and tasted hot peppers. We milked Brownie and mowed the field with a scythe.

In the evening, while Grandma and Grandpa rested on the porch, we caught lightning bugs in the field with Daddy. We put them in jars with holes in the top and made our own flashlights.

One night Daddy taught us a game called "devil and the pies" that he had played when he was a little boy. Brian was the "devil." Gary, Kevin, and I were "pies." And Daddy was the "door." The door gave each of us pies a secret flavor. "You're sweet potato, and you're apple, and you're cherry," my father whispered.

"Knock, knock," said the devil.

"What do you want?" asked the door.

"I want a pie!" the devil said, smacking his lips.

"What flavor?" the door demanded.

The devil thought for a moment, then answered, "Uh…apple!"

I was the apple pie! The devil chased me as I ran through the field in the dark, trying not to get caught. The door was home base— Daddy was reaching out for me. "Safe!"

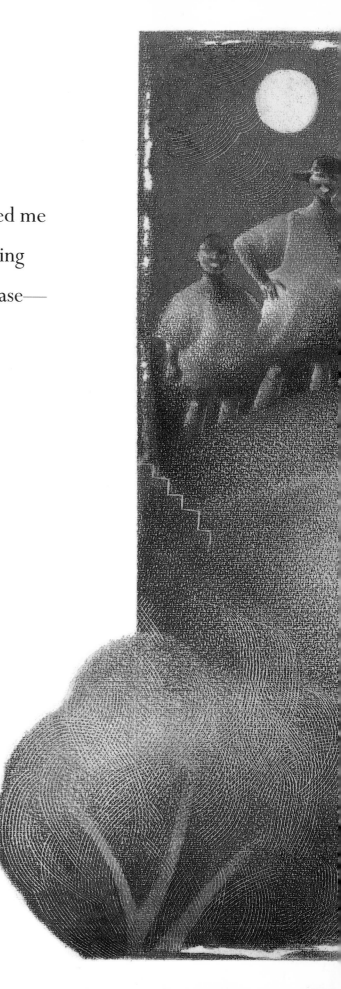

"Bedtime, sleepyheads," said Daddy. He gave Kevin a piggyback ride and held Brian's hand while Gary and I trailed behind up the stairs. Daddy shared the extra bedroom with my brothers. Since I was the oldest, I slept on a cot in the hallway.

"What's that?" I whispered, seeing a strange shape on my window. "It looks like a hand."

"Not a hand, sugar," said Daddy, tucking me in. "Just some candle flies. They like the light. But then they fly away. See?" He tapped the pane and the hand disappeared.

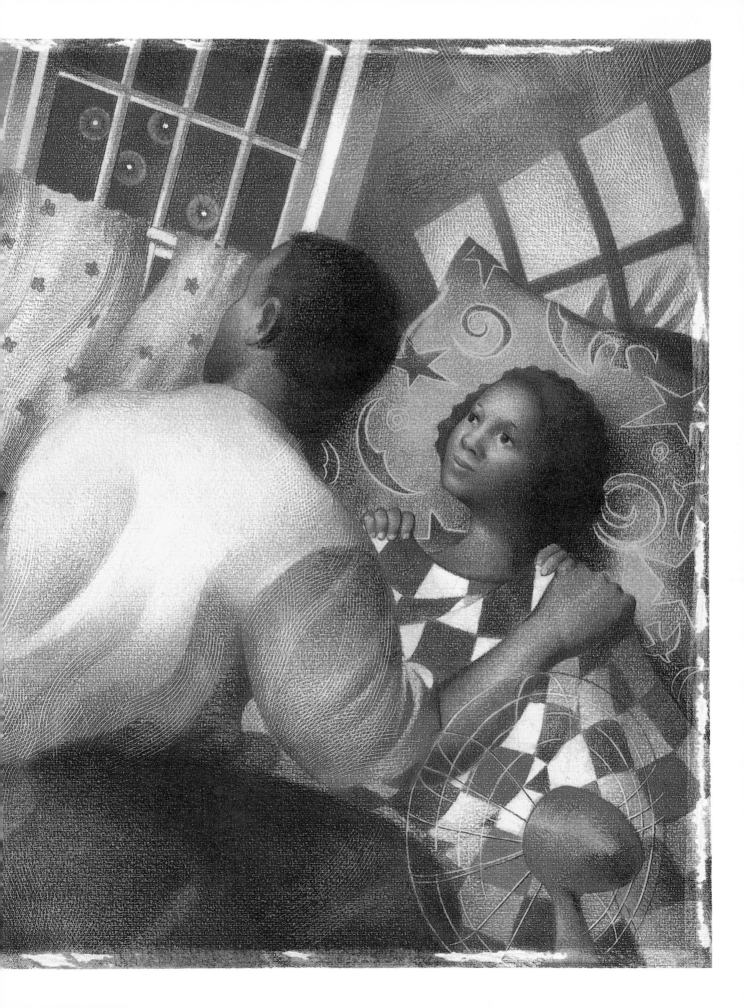

One morning Daddy announced, "Let's go for a treat." We put on our shoes to walk to the general store. Sitting down on high stools, we drank grape soda. The storekeeper, whose name was Bernice, called it "soda pop."

"Tomorrow I'm leaving," Daddy told us.

"How come?" I asked him, trying not to cry.

"I've been having a problem getting my life together," Daddy said quietly. "Now, at least, I've got a new job. I'll be driving a truck cross-country. Maybe someday I won't have to go.

"I'll be thinking of you."

"You're always going somewhere!" grumbled Gary.

"Can't we come with you?" asked Brian. "Please, Dad."

Daddy shook his head no. "You're better off with your mom, having a regular life," he said.

"When am I going to see you again?" I asked him.

"Soon," he promised. He hugged me. "I love you. Just remember, wherever I am, I'm always your dad."

During the leftover summer days, Gary, Brian, Kevin, and I played and did our chores. At night we listened to peepers with Grandma and Grandpa. Sometimes there was a moon with no stars in the sky. Sometimes there was a moon and stars together. Once, all by itself, was the biggest moon I'd ever seen. It was round and orange and looked like a sweet-potato pie.

I don't dream much, but every once in a while I do have one. Back home in the city, Mom comes into my room when she hears me wake up. "What is it, sugar?" she asks me. When I tell her what I dreamed about, it is always the same....

I am standing in the field with Daddy. There are lots of stars in the sky and a moon the color of sweet potato. And fluttering all around are silvery candle flies.

Wherever he is, I know my dad loves me. He's always my dad.